Derick's Gem

By David Evans

One day Derrick was sitting beside his mother while she was doing the laundry.

I know that you want to go outside, we’ll go out soon.

You haven’t taken me to see the cave or even to the zoo in a while.

Your father and I have been very busy for days, as he let out a yawn.

Tomorrow we're going to the Grand Canyon, I've always wanted to know what was at the bottom of it.

You can't go down there, it's too dangerous.

Our uncle went down there, that's because he's a park Ranger and can handle any terrain.

“Do you think I'll ever be able to climb a mountain?”

“You will, just give it time.”

“Did I tell you about your aunt’s surprise?”

“No,” you didn't.

“Is it another stuffed animal?”

“No.”

If I told you, then I would ruin the surprise.

Then his mother’s cell phone rang, she got up and quickly went into the other room.

Derick took out the legos from under his bed and began putting them together.

The family's dog came into the room, his name is Tim.

Tim went over to Derek and dropped his ball next to him.

I know that you want me to throw your ball, but I can't trust you not running away.

I'm sure my dad will take you out later on, he began giving him kisses on his face.

Don't be silly, you can stop kissing me now.

Tim walked out of his room and went down the hallway.

Sometime later his mother came back, with a serious look on her face.

Derick went to his mother and sat down.

Your aunt was in a bad accident, her car is totaled.

The other driver passed away at the scene.

"Did an Angel take him away?"

"I sure hope so."

I wish that no more accidents happened, I do too but they happen.

"When is she going to be better?"

"It depends on, how bad she got hurt."

"Are we going to pray for her?"

"Yes," we will. I wish I could cheer her up

You can once she's better. I've decided to let the babysitter, take you to the Grand Canyon.

"What if something happens?"

"Nothing is going to happen either one of you."

You'll have to be on your best behavior, you know that I will be.

I packed you a nice lunch, in your lunch box, your dad and I will be back as soon as we can.

After we leave the hospital, were going to have to drive to another state to help your brother move.

I don't know why you didn't mention that to me any sooner because we forgot.

His mother kissed him on the forehead, and his father walked into the room and gave him a hug.

I know that you don't like the babysitter but you can put up with it.

We hope that you have a good time at the Grand Canyon, just then the babysitter Lauren walked in.

His parents waved goodbye and dashed out the door.

His mother came back inside and instructed the babysitter and walked out.

Every time that I see you, you grow a little more.

“Aren’t you going to turn 10 on July 15?”

“Yes,” but I'm not looking forward to it.

“Why are you so down about it?”

“My friend won’t be coming to visit me on my birthday.”

I'm sure that you're going to get many presents, but it won't help my aunt get better.

“What happened to her?”

“She was in a bad car accident.”

You shouldn’t be worried about everything, just try to be a kid for once.

I’m sure I can make something out of these legos faster that you can, then Tim walked into the room.

I missed petting your dog, I hope that we're going to do something more interesting than just talking.

Yes, we most certainly will, I'm just catching up on everything.

“Did your mother pack your lunch?”

“Yes.”

I’m going to go grab your lunch, along with my purse and we can go.

“Do you think Tim will be okay, until we get back home?”

“Yes,” he’ll be just fine.

“Now what are you doing?”

“Taking bottles of water out of the refrigerator.”

You're lucky because I remembered the sunscreen, she handed him a bottle of water.

Neither one of us are going to get dehydrated out there.

I've never seen this vehicle before, it's because I just bought it two days ago.

He quickly got into the back of the car, and strapped himself in.

You strap yourself in like an old pro, that's because my dad taught me how.

My daughter just turned 25 yesterday, she's doing great in college.

“Would you like me to put the radio on?”

“No.”

“Are we going to leave now?”

“Yes,” we are.

Then her cell phone fell down out of the car, she reached down and picked it up.

She closed her door and put the car into reverse.

Don't worry your little self, I'm going to turn on the air conditioning.

They left the driveway and now we're on to the road.

The last time I drove you, you kept asking me are we there yet.

I swear that you were possessed that afternoon, I just ate too many candy bars that day.

"Have you ever met my uncle?"

"No," I haven't.

The light turned red and they came to a stop, a few kids and an elderly man crossed the street.

Then a mother duck and her ducklings crossed the street.

The light turned green and they were off, those ducklings that crossed the street sure were cute.

I wish I could have seen them, me too.

Derek looked out the window and saw an airplane flying along, through the puffy clouds.

"Have you ever rode in an airplane?"

"Yes," plenty of times.

"Haven't you?"

“No.”

You're still just a little boy, you will when you’re grown.

Suddenly a car swerved towards them going into their lane, Lauren quickly maneuvered the car out of the way.

“Are you okay?”

“Yes,” I am.

You really handled what just happened, really well.

Things like that have happened to me, many times while on the road.

“Do you recognize the road that we're on?”

“Yes,” I do.

They passed the rest stop, we're almost there. Derick stretched his arms out and yawned.

A car quickly sped past them; I can't believe that man just sped past us like that.

On the right side of the road Derek saw a sign that said homemade ice cream made here.

“Did you see the ice cream shop back there?”

“No,” I'm too busy driving.

An ambulance came speeding up the road behind them, she quickly got over letting the ambulance pass by.

“Why did you do that for?”

“Because it’s what you have to do when you see an ambulance coming.”

If you don't give them their space, then you'll get a fine.

There was a detour sign up, hold on we're going to go down a bumpy road.

The potholes on this road aren't very kind to vehicles, you don't have to worry I'm used to going over bumpy roads.

I can't wait until I'm old enough to go mudding, I heard that it's a lot of fun to go off road and a truck.

It’s a lot of fun but you're going to get stuck, but that's the best part.

You're just a typical boy who likes mud, I grew up with my sister who thought that she was a Princess.

Eventually they got to the parks visitor center, I don't want you to lean over any railings.

I won't risk letting you fall and try to follow close behind me.

“Did you drink your water already?”

“Yes.”

It's quite unusual that there aren't many people here right now, and that's probably because today is such a hot day.

The sun was high in the sky, and there was a slight breeze going.

They went over to the Ranger station; the Ranger was sitting on a stool going through paperwork.

"Excuse me Sir is the park open?"

"Yes," it is.

The Rangers eyes were bleary eyed, and he was yawning.

You look like, you have been up for days.

This place has been crazy for the last two nights, people were fighting and setting off fireworks.

If I wouldn't have stayed here I can't imagine what would have happened to this park.

> "How long are the two of you planning to stay here?"
>
> "An hour or two."

> "Did you hear about the earthquake that happened here last week?"

> "No," we didn't.

I was sitting here and suddenly the ground shook beneath me.

“Can we walk around soon?”

“Yes,” after this gentleman and I are done talking.

Sometimes he gets just a little impatient, that's quite alright.

When I was that age it was difficult for my mother to keep track of me, I was always getting into something.

Lucky for me when I was young, there was no internet.

I was always running around with the other kids, some days we would get together and play football.

It sounds like you have had a good childhood.

In the middle of the afternoon yesterday I saw a bald eagle fly over.

Derick grew bored and wandered away.

He was headed for the gift shop, there were three people standing by the door.

They all peered over at him, while he was entering the shop.

There was a tall man standing behind the counter, staring into his phone.

There were all kinds of books stacked up on the shelf in the back of the place.

There were balloons next to the stuffed animals, and there were tour maps.

When Lauren looked down and didn't see Derick, she got all beside herself.

I’ll be cutting our conversation short; I have to go find him now.

I'll gladly help you look for him, no but thanks for the offer.

She feverishly went running, she called his name several times but he still didn't come out.

She thought to herself he never makes things easy for me.

People were giving her all kinds of looks, I'm just looking around for the kid, she heard someone say your irresponsible.

The woman gave her a dirty look and walked away.

She kept looking around and finally decided to go in the gift shop, excuse me.

The man was too busy looking into his phone to hear her, I said hello.

The men finally heard her and put his phone down.

"'What do you need help with today?"

"Finding my boy."

"Have you saw him?"

"No," I didn't.

There have been many children in here in the past hour, she angrily said I guess people don't look around these days.

If I lose him his parents will never forgive me, I'm sorry ma'am.

Just go back to what you were doing, I'm not stopping until I find him.

Meanwhile, Derick's uncle had taken them on a helicopter ride.

I didn't know that you were a helicopter pilot too, yes and I love to fly.

We really should have told my babysitter that we were doing this, oh don't worry about her.

She's probably going to call the police soon, then you're going to get in trouble.

There was a flock of birds coming towards them, hold on we have to maneuver around these birds.

"What happens if we hit the birds?"

"They could cause us to crash."

This thing only has one engine and if it goes out we're going to crash.

It takes a lot of skill to fly helicopter around these canyons, if you look away for a moment you may crash.

It took me years of flying to get this good, I still have had some close calls though.

My family doesn't like the fact that I'm still flying, they think I'm going to crash.

I think that you're the coolest uncle in the whole wide world, you always know how to cheer me up.

"Are we going to land soon?"

"Yes," we are.

Eventually they landed at the bottom of the Canyon, getting lost down here could prove fatal.

“What kind of animal do you think those bones belong to over there?”

“An unlucky bison that fell down here.”

Get away from those bones, we're not paleontologists.

“What does that big word mean.”

“It's someone who studies ancient fossils.”

We need to move on now, come with me down this path.

We don't have much further to go, I'm sure you're wondering where the path to the left goes.

We'll discuss that later, for now we have some digging to do.

He pointed out to Derek where they're going to dig, this doesn't seem like too much fun to me.

It'll be worth it in the end, once we both start digging it won't take us long.

"What's the coolest thing that you have dug up?"

"A gem, and a ring someone lost."

I sold the ring a while ago, on the internet.

“Are you sure we can keep what we find down here?”

“Yes,” and no one needs to know that we found anything down here.

But you know I want to tell my parents where I found it.

If I were you I would just make up a story, but then I wouldn't be telling the truth.

They kept on digging, until they came upon a bone.

This is just a bone from an animal, just toss it aside.

“Why’d you stop digging?”

“I thought I heard something coming from that way.”

“From the left or right of us?”

“The left.”

“Is this place haunted?”

“No,” not that I know of.

They dug on tirelessly and came upon 3 gems.

His uncle began jumping up and down, were rich at last.

Pick the gem that you want, the gems are pretty much the same size.

There's a reddish one, a purple one and yellow one.

I'd like the red one, that's a great choice. Derick picked it up and put it in his pocket.

While the babysitter was sitting patiently on the bench, by the Ranger station.

Just then the sky began to cloud up, by the look of the sky we better get out of here.

Make sure that you didn't leave anything behind, I didn't.

"Do you remember which way to get out of here?"

"Yes," I do.

While they were walking along his uncle tripped over a stone.

He carefully got himself to his feet with, the help from Derek.

They soon came upon the helicopter, and quickly got in it and strapped themselves in.

His uncle started it up, and they were now making their way out of the canyon.

I'm hoping that we can get out of here before the storm hits.

Within no time, they were back where they started.

Once his uncle got out of the helicopter, he made a dash for his car.

The moment that Lauren saw him she began to cry, thank goodness you're okay.

> "I was looking in the dirt with my uncle for gems.

> "Where were you doing that?"

> "Somewhere near the Canyon."

> "Where's your uncle at right now?"

"He went back to his car, and probably left by now."

Let's get you back to the car and we're going home, you haven't been good all day.

If your parents saw you like this, they'd probably keep you in timeout for days.

They both got in the car, closing the doors behind them.

They put on their seatbelts and away they went.

After a long car ride, Derek was home safe and sound.

An hour later his parents returned, the babysitter told them about what happened and left.

He showed his parents the gem that he had found, and they held a nice conversation. Later that evening, they tucked him into bed.

www.ingramcontent.com/pod-product-compliance
Lightning Source LLC
LaVergne TN
LVHW040932150826
845672LV00007B/2329